BOOMER EXPLORES ANNAPOLIS

Written by Angelique Clarke
Illustrated by Jim Hunt

4880 Lower Valley Road Atglen, Pennsylvania 19310

Printed in China

DEDICATION
For My Family

Other Schiffer Books on Related Subjects:
Greetings from Annapolis, 0-7643-2600-7, $19.95
Annapolis Vignettes, 978-0-8703-3571-6, $24.95

Type set in Comic Sans
ISBN: 978-0-7643-4008-6
Printed in China

Schiffer Books are available at special discounts for bulk purchases for sales promotions or premiums. Special editions, including personalized covers, corporate imprints, and excerpts can be created in large quantities for special needs. For more information contact the publisher:

Published by Schiffer Publishing Ltd.
4880 Lower Valley Road
Atglen, PA 19310
Phone: (610) 593-1777; Fax: (610) 593-2002
E-mail: Info@schifferbooks.com

For the largest selection of fine reference books on this and related subjects, please visit our website at
www.schifferbooks.com
We are always looking for people to write books on new and related subjects. If you have an idea for a book, please contact us at
proposals@schifferbooks.com

This book may be purchased from the publisher.
Include $5.00 for shipping.
Please try your bookstore first.
You may write for a free catalog.

In Europe, Schiffer books are distributed by
Bushwood Books
6 Marksbury Ave.
Kew Gardens
Surrey TW9 4JF England
Phone: 44 (0) 20 8392 8585; Fax: 44 (0) 20 8392 9876
E-mail: info@bushwoodbooks.co.uk
Website: www.bushwoodbooks.co.uk

Boomer is a silly dog who loves to explore.

One day when the garden gate is mysteriously left open, he cannot resist darting out of the yard, dashing up the street, and embarking on an exciting adventure through his hometown.

Boomer lives in Annapolis, Maryland.

He loves his town and all the sites and history that goes with it.

BUT he especially loves Bridget, who he spends his days with.

...And Bridget loves Boomer.

So when she discovers Boomer is missing, she quickly picks up her phone and calls everyone she knows, hoping someone has seen him.

Boomer ZOOMS down Duke of Gloucester Street and quickly turns the corner before anyone can see him...

...Or so he thinks.

"Hey Coach, isn't that Boomer?! Blow your whistle!"

"Hoot, Hoot!"

"He's heading toward the Charles Carroll House."

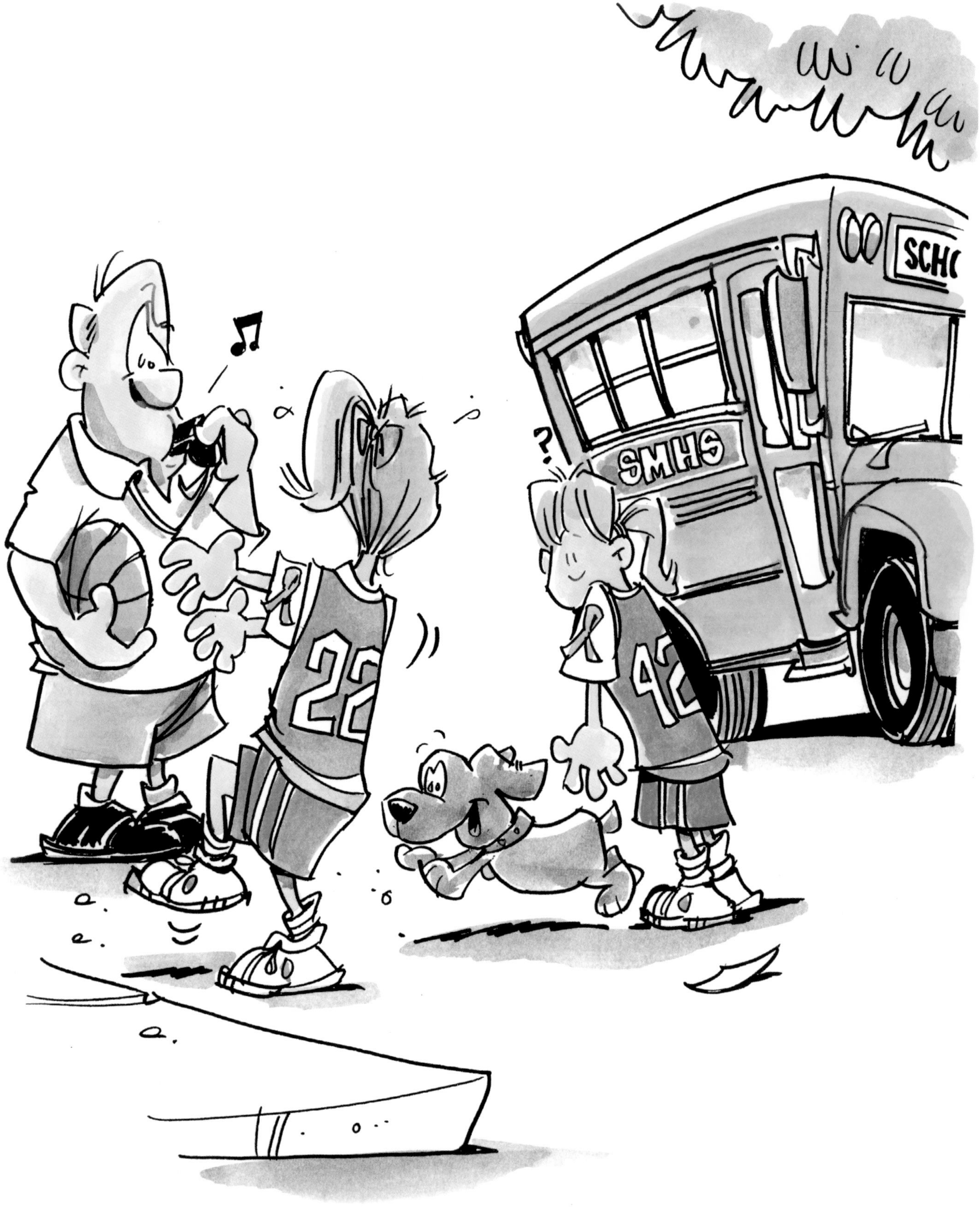
SCHO
SMHS
22
42

Boomer knows that Charles Carroll was one of four Marylanders to sign the Declaration of Independence. He learns today that he was born right here in this house.

Just then a cat zips by — and Boomer runs off to play.

"BEEP, BEEP!"

Bridget receives a text from the Town Crier.

She opens her phone and reads the message:

DID YOU KNOW?
Squire Frederick is the official Town Crier for the City of Annapolis. This is a lifetime appointment.

The ducks are too fast for Boomer at the City Dock, so he sits and watches the boats sail by. There are so many!

"Is this why Annapolis is referred to as Americas Sailing Capital?" Boomer wonders.

DID YOU KNOW?
Annapolis City Dock is the site of Kunta Kinte's arrival to America. This is memorialized by a statue of Author and Historian Alex Haley located in downtown Annapolis at City Dock.

By the time Bridget gets to the City Dock, Boomer is nowhere to be found. She knows he will be getting hungry soon and there is only one place in town he will go for food.

So, Bridget decides to go and wait for Boomer there.

Boomer roams Main, Francis, and Pinkney Streets.

He darts around Church and State Circles, two times each!

He barks up Prince and howls down King, George Streets that is... just because he can!

He stops for water at the local shop, sniffs flowers in the beautiful gardens, and chases croquet balls on the lawn of St. Johns College.

Soon, Boomer is exhausted!

He plops down on the grass in front of a huge building with a dome on top. This must be the State House, he thinks to himself.

Boomer knows that Annapolis is the capital of Maryland, but he learns today that Annapolis also served as the capital of the entire United States from November 1783 until August 1784.

DID YOU KNOW?
The dome of the Annapolis Capital has no nails! It is held together by wooden pegs and iron straps.

Boomer is hungry!

All this exploring sure has made his tummy grumble — and he hasn't even made it to the United States Naval Academy yet.

He heads toward Maryland Avenue.

DID YOU KNOW?
The United States Naval Academy was founded in 1845. The Naval Academy first accepted women as midshipmen in 1976.

Maryland Avenue is one of Boomer's favorite places to explore. The friendly shopkeepers in their quaint shops always have a treat or a belly rub waiting for him.

And today would be no different...

TO: BOOMER
FROM:
MISS PEGGY

Boomer is the happiest dog in Annapolis!

But wait!

He sure does miss Bridget! Then, he hears a familiar voice...

"Boomer! I thought you might show up here!"

Bridget scoops Boomer up and gives him a great big hug!

"Where have you been? Another one of your adventures? What did you see today?"

Boomer licks Bridget... He is ready to go home.

Boomer knows that there is still a lot more to see and explore in Annapolis... but it will have to wait for another day.

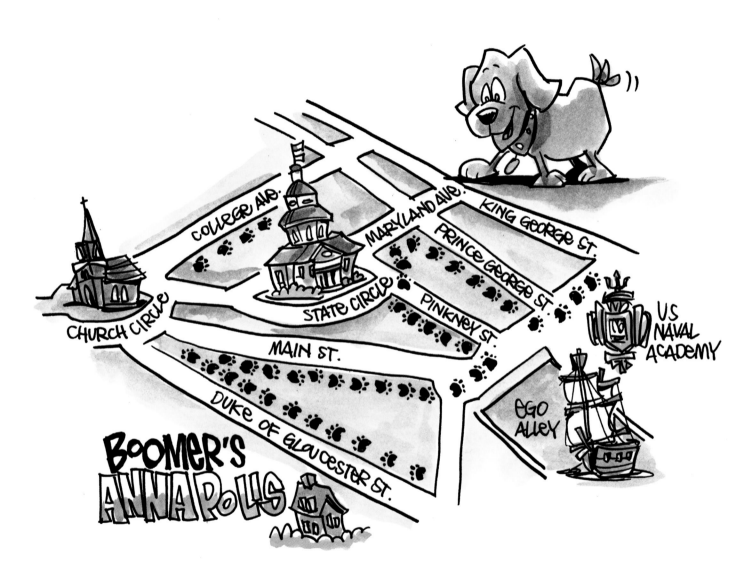